I'll Love You Always

Mark Sperring
&
Alison Brown

BLOOMSBURY
LONDON OXFORD NEW YORK NEW DELHI SYDNEY

How long will I love you?
A second is too short.
A second is no time
for a love of this sort.

A minute is no better, for minutes fly by!

They're gone in a moment like a sweet butterfly.

An hour's still nothing –
it whirls by so fast.

I'll love you much longer than hours can last.

A morning is so brief,
an afternoon, too.

From sunrise to sunset,
I'll keep loving you.

Will I love you when night falls?

Of course, and beyond . . .

Will I love you tomorrow?
Oh yes, on and on . . .

I'll love you for whole days
stretched out in a line.

I'll love you for weeks
and a much longer time!

I'll love you for months
heaped up to the sky.

I'll love you through seasons
as they bluster by.

I'll love you for whole years
and though things might change . . .
as you grow bigger
my love stays the same.

How long will I love you?
If you need to know,
I'll tuck you in tightly,
then whisper it low . . .

I'll love you for years and for months, weeks and days. I'll love you for hours and minutes

. . . always.

I'll love you forever, not one second less.
For that is what mummies and daddies do best.